Milo's Tale

Kay Cochran Albright
Illustrated by Emmi Harding

Outskirts Press, Inc.
http://www.outskirtspress.com

Paperback ISBN: 978-1-4787-7402-0

Illustrations by: Emmi Harding. All rights reserved - used with permission.

Outskirts Press and the "OP" logo are trademarks belonging to Outskirts Press, Inc.

PRINTED IN THE UNITED STATES OF AMERICA

This Book Belongs to:

This book is dedicated to my daughter,
Lauren Albright Burch.
She has been my primary caretaker;
I love her so much!

A big thank you for all the
love and support of my family and friends
who have surrounded me on this journey…
So much love to my son, Sam Albright,
my son-in-law, Connor Burch,
my first grandchild, Evelyn McKay, and
my future grandchildren!

Our "Dottiemom" is greatly appreciated for
making this book possible and
bringing so much joy to every day.

Lastly, to all the families fighting ALS and
their caretakers. We are all in this together.

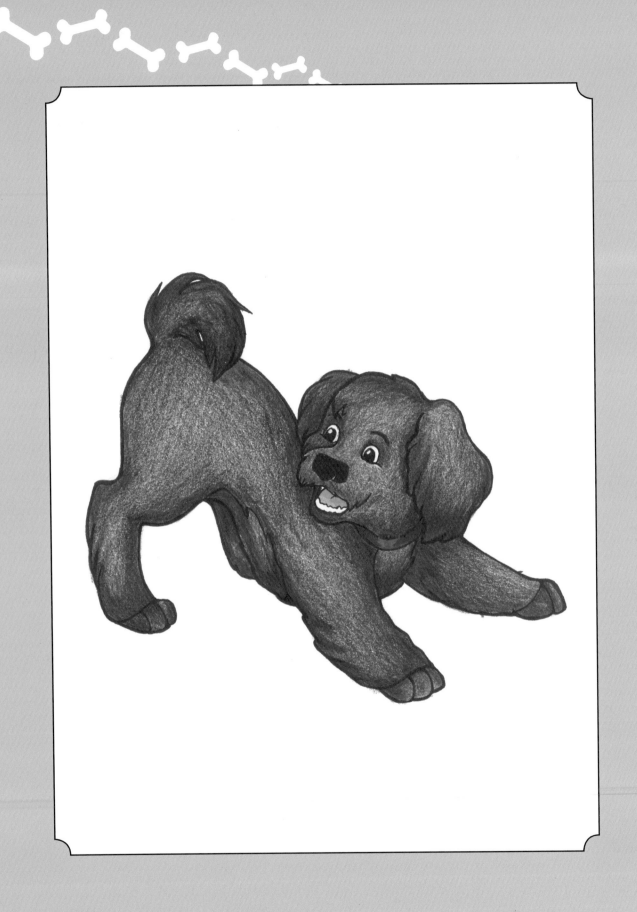

H i, I'm Milo and this is my tail.

Well, this is my tale...

W hen I was born I was the runt of the litter.

That means I was the smallest of all my brothers and sisters.

As they got bigger and played harder, I couldn't keep up.

Once we were old enough it was time for all of us to go to adopted homes.

I watched as one by one my brothers and sisters went to new homes.

It didn't look like anyone would ever want me.

Then, one day, I saw someone who looked very different.

Instead of walking in, she sat in a chair that moved.

And that's not all!

She had a computer in front of her.

Her voice did not come from her mouth; it came from the computer.

She was strange looking, but she seemed nice.

She was looking for a dog that could sit in her lap.

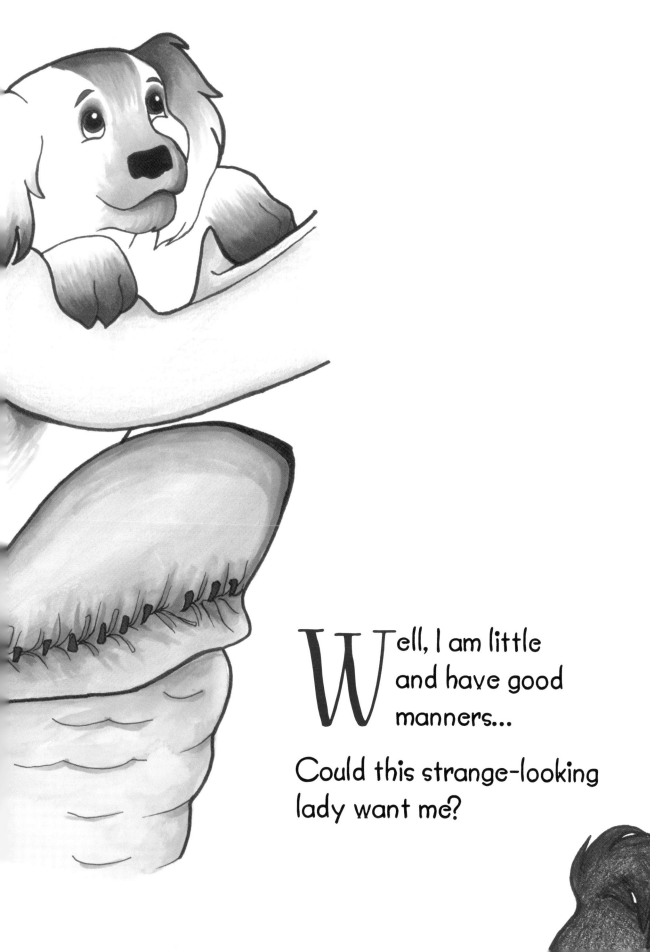

W ell, I am little and have good manners...

Could this strange-looking lady want me?

There were other puppies in the room, though.

Oh, no! They were bigger and played more than me.

Out of nowhere the strange-looking lady's daughter, Lauren, picked me up and put me in her lap!

Oh, what a feeling. This is where I belong!

Please pick me,

pick me,

me, me!

Guess what?
You guessed it.... She picked me!

I was going to have a family, a home,
and a lap.

A lap that moved!

Oh boy,

oh boy,

oh boy!

W

hen we got home I met my new family.

I was very shy, but I felt safe in my mom's lap.

Well, there was a lot of talk about my name.

So, my name is not runt.

They finally decided...

I have a name!

I have a name!

And it's,

it's MILO!

I AM

M - I - L - O...

MILO!

It didn't take long before I learned more about my new family.

Mom has something called ALS.

It's what the famous baseball player, Lou Gehrig, had.

So she cannot move her body anymore.

And the moving chair is a wheelchair.

I have a name, a home, and a job!

My job is to love and comfort my mom.

The best job ever!

Since my mom cannot move I snuggle my mom.

Snuggle, snuggle,

snuggle.

I love snuggles!

Do you?

Oh boy,

oh boy, oh boy,

I love snuggles!

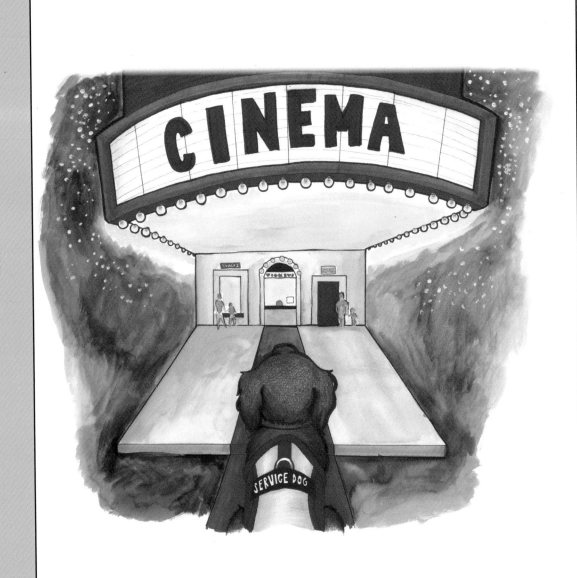

W
e go out a lot.

Since I have an important job I get to go everywhere Mom goes.

Even to the movies!

And you know what that means...

Guess! Guess!

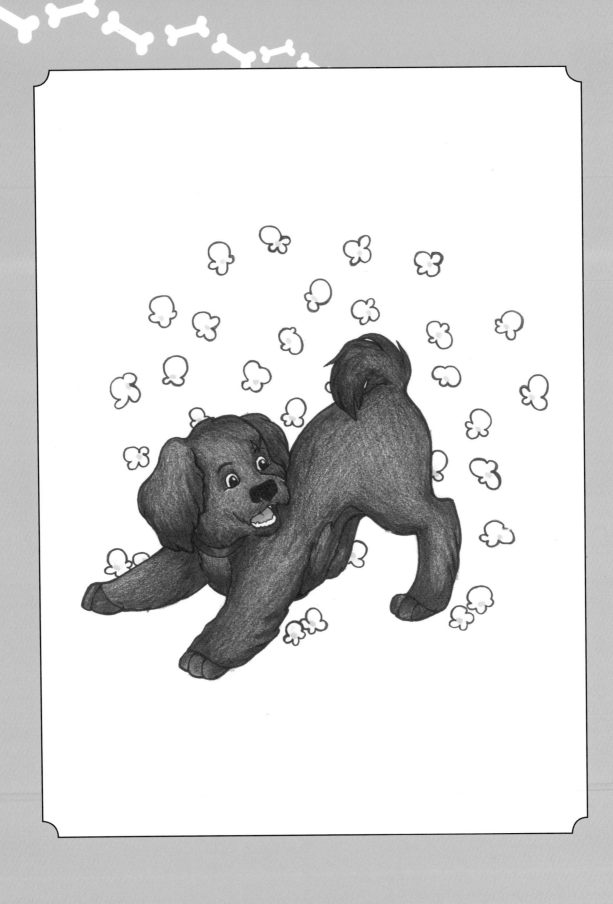

Y ou guessed it!
POPCORN!

Oh boy,

oh boy,

oh boy!

I love popcorn!

We go to stores a lot, too.

Y ou know what I see?

I see a lot of people looking at my mom.

I see people stare, point, look away, and even look scared!

Scared of my sweet mom?

People should see other people the way dogs see people.

W e don't see the way they look on the outside.

We see from the inside.

We see kind, sweet, friendly, and loving.

We do not care how people look.

And, of course, we all like snuggles.

Oh, I did not tell you. I live on a farm.

M om and I love to go to the barn!

Oh boy,

oh boy,

oh boy!

I love the barn!

M om has had her horse, Sam, for a long time.

He knows she can no longer pet him.

So he pets her by touching her face with his nose.

Sam knows she is the same on the inside, even if she looks different on the outside.

So horses can snuggle, too.

Oh boy,

oh boy,

oh boy!

Everybody loves

snuggles!

Some people with ALS have problems breathing.

So Mom was too.

She could get help breathing by putting a tube in her throat.

Mom had to stay in a hospital to get the tube.

So guess what?

You guessed it.

I got to go, too!

Everyone was nice.

A lot of people came in the room just to see me!

I think it is because I have such an important job.

Snuggling my mom.

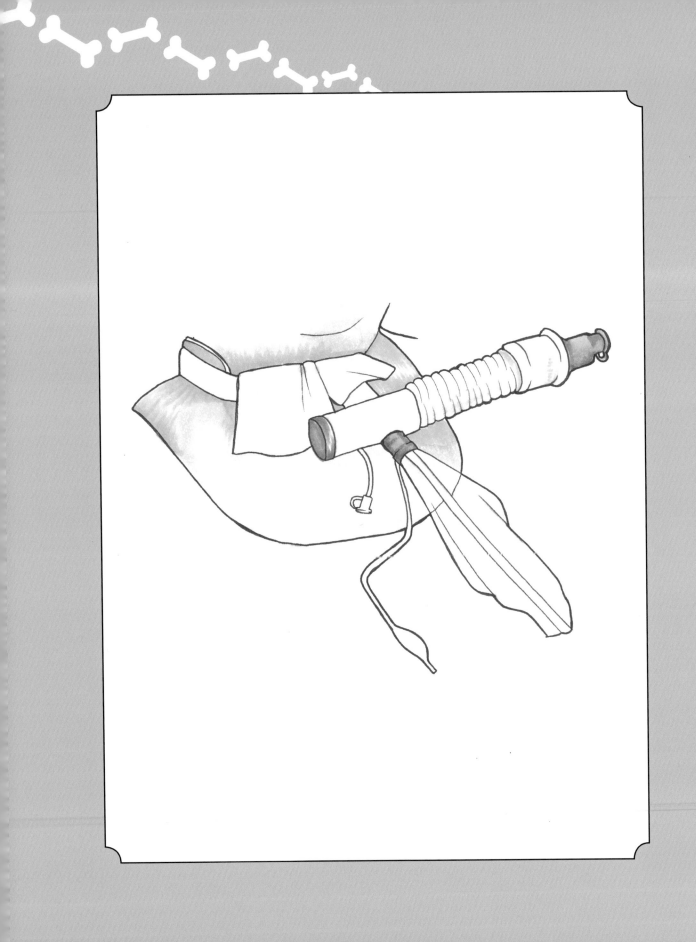

If you see someone with a tube attached to their neck, it is to help them breathe.

There is nothing to be afraid of.

Just smile and say hey.

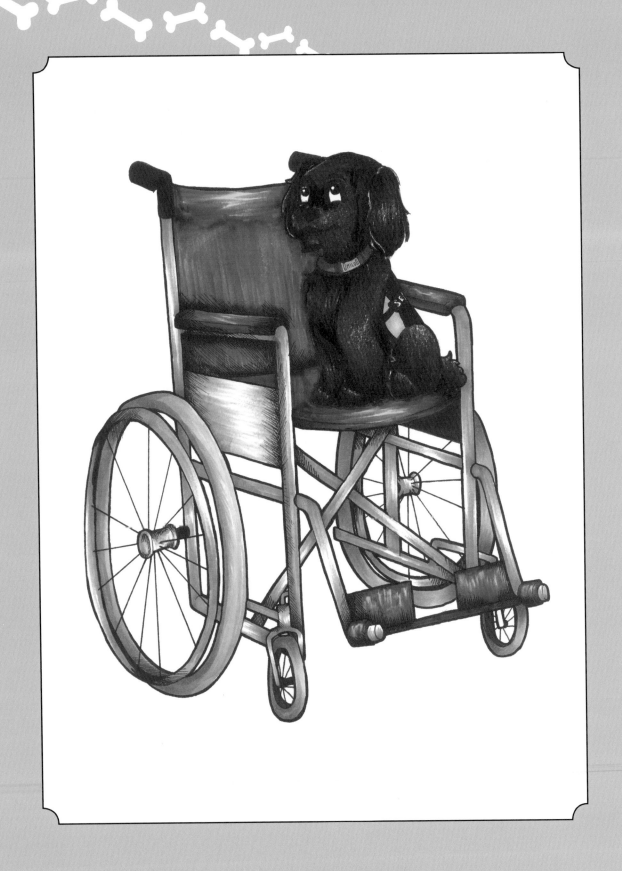

D o you know anyone who is in a wheelchair or that looks different from you?

Just remember to be kind and loving.

What really matters comes from the inside of a person, not the outside.

Look at people the way dogs do.

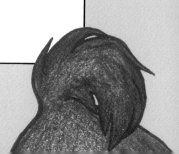

O

f course, never forget to snuggle, snuggle, snuggle!

Oh boy,

oh boy,

oh boy!

EVERYONE LOVES SNUGGLES!

"About the Author"

Kay grew up on a Georgia farm and graduated from the University of Georgia in 1980. Prior to her ALS diagnosis Kay was an active and healthy realtor. She was always on the go and smiling. Kay was diagnosed with ALS in February of 2011. From the day of her diagnosis she decided she was going to make the most of every day and do all that was in her power to contribute to ALS research and awareness. She loves her two wonderful children, animals, and is very excited about her first grandchild, Evvy McKay, due in October 2016.

"About the Illustrator"

Emmi Harding is currently a sophomore at the University of Georgia studying drawing and painting. She was immediately interested in illustrating this book because her grandfather passed away due to ALS before she was born. She hopes that this book will raise awareness of this illness and help to promote research for a cure.

About ALS

ALS is often called Lou Gehrig's Disease.

Lou Gehrig's Disease damages motor neurons in the brain and spinal cord. Motor neurons are the nerve cells that control muscle movement.

When ALS attacks a body it causes the motor neurons to shrink and disappear, which means muscles no longer receive signals to move. Over time the body will become paralyzed, meaning the muscles no longer work.

Even when someone with ALS loses their ability to move their muscles, all their senses still work, including their brain.

There is no known cause or cure for ALS.

Kay describes ALS as "being buried alive in my own body. My mind is the same, my senses are the same, I can feel everything. I just cannot move!"

For more information about ALS
visit http://kidshealth.org/en/kids/als.html

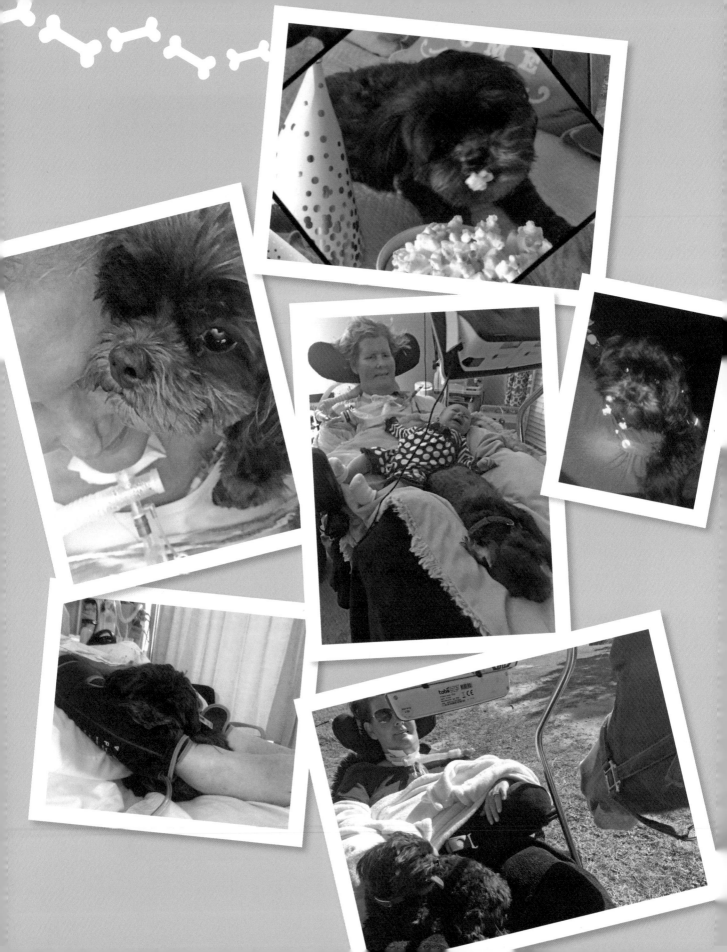

CPSIA information can be obtained at www.ICGtesting.com
Printed in the USA
LVIW01n0212310117
522661LV00005B/15